Cows in the Kitchen

illustrated by Airlie Anderson

Child's Play (International) Ltd
Ashworth Rd, Bridgemead, Swindon SN5 7YD, UK
Swindon Auburn ME Sydney
ISBN 978-1-84643-621-5 L2410228X812226215

Printed in Heshan, China
5 7 9 10 8 6 4
www.childs-play.com

Cows in the kitchen, **Moo Moo Moo!**
Cows in the kitchen, **Moo Moo Moo!**
Cows in the kitchen, **Moo Moo Moo!**
What shall we do, Tom Farmer?

Ducks in the dishes, **Quack Quack Quack!**
Ducks in the dishes, **Quack Quack Quack!**
Ducks in the dishes, **Quack Quack Quack!**
What shall we do, Tom Farmer?

Cats in the cupboard, doggies
Cats in the cupboard, doggies
Cats in the cupboard, doggies
What shall we do, Tom Farme

Sheep in the shower, **Baa Baa Baa!**
Sheep in the shower, **Baa Baa Baa!**
Sheep in the shower, **Baa Baa Baa!**
What shall we do, Tom Farmer?

Pigs in the garden, **Oink Oink Oink!**
Pigs in the garden, **Oink Oink Oink!**
Pigs in the garden, **Oink Oink Oink!**
What shall we do, Tom Farmer?

Goats in the greenhouse, **Meh Meh Meh!**
Goats in the greenhouse, **Meh Meh Meh!**
Goats in the greenhouse, **Meh Meh Meh!**
What shall we do, Tom Farmer?

Chase them away, **Shoo Shoo Shoo!**
Chase them away, **Shoo Shoo Shoo!**
Chase them away, **Shoo Shoo Shoo!**
That's what we'll do, Tom Farmer!

Woof!
Woof!
Woof!
Oink!
Oink!
Oink!
Meh!
Meh!
Meh!
Moo!
Moo!
Moo!
Quack!
Quack!
Quack
Baa!
Baa!
Baa!
Miaow!
Miaow!
Miaow